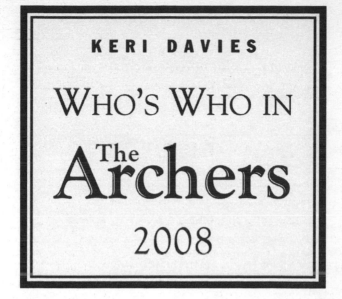

KERI DAVIES

WHO'S WHO IN

The Archers

2008

D0280211

BBC
BOOKS

To Betty, an example to us all.

1 3 5 7 9 10 8 6 4 2

This book is published to accompany the BBC Radio 4 serial *The Archers*. The editor of *The Archers* is Vanessa Whitburn.

Published in 2007 by BBC Books, an imprint of Ebury Publishing. Ebury Publishing is a division of the Random House Group Ltd.

The Random House Group Limited Reg. No. 954009.
Addresses for companies within the Random House Group can be found at www.randomhouse.co.uk

A CIP catalogue record for this book is available from the British Library.

ISBN 978 1 84607 326 7

The Random House Group Limited makes every effort to ensure that the papers used in our books are made from trees that have been legally sourced from well-managed and credibly certified forests. Our paper procurement policy can be found at www.randomhouse.co.uk

Commissioning editor: Mathew Clayton
Project editor: Steve Tribe

Typeset in Garamond Light
Printed and bound in Great Britain by Cox & Wyman Ltd, Reading, Berkshire.

To buy books by your favourite authors and register for offers, visit www. rbooks.co.uk

Events in Ambridge are constantly changing, but we have done our best to make *Who's Who in The Archers 2008* accurate at the time of publication.

Official Archers Website: bbc.co.uk/radio4/archers, to listen again to *Archers* episodes, including an audio archive of the last seven days. The site also features daily plot synopses, news, information, a map of Ambridge, a detailed timeline, archive moments, quizzes and chat.

Official Fan Club: Archers Addicts
01789 207480 www.archers-addicts.com

THE AUTHOR
A former senior producer of *The Archers*, Keri Davies became an Archers scriptwriter in 2003 and runs the *Archers* website. He lives in Birmingham with his wife and three sons and is a part-time drummer and DJ, so it's amazing that he's got any hearing left.

WELCOME TO AMBRIDGE

This is the ninth edition of our handy guide to the characters and locations in *The Archers*.

It has been an eventful year in Ambridge – but when was it ever otherwise? This update reflects major stories such as the tumultuous arrival of Brian's love child at Home Farm and the halting recovery of David and Ruth's marriage. But it also takes into account the lighter side, including the triumphant pancake race victory of our yummy mummy, Sabrina Thwaite.

Yes, all human life is here...

Vanessa Whitburn
Editor, The Archers

FREQUENTLY ASKED QUESTIONS

When and how can I hear the programme?

On BBC Radio 4 (92–95 FM, 198 LW and on digital radio and television). Transmission times: 7pm Sunday to Friday, repeated at 2pm the next day (excluding Saturdays). An omnibus edition of the whole week's episodes is broadcast every Sunday at 10am. It can also be heard worldwide up to seven days after transmission via *The Archers* website: bbc.co.uk/radio4/archers.

How many people listen?

Nearly five million every week in the UK alone. *The Archers* is the most popular non-news programme on BBC Radio 4, and the most listened-to BBC programme online.

How long has it been going?

Five pilot episodes were broadcast on the BBC Midlands Home Service in Whit Week 1950, but *The Archers*' first national broadcast was on 1 January 1951. Episode 15,360, broadcast on 1 January 2008, makes this comfortably the world's longest-running radio drama.

How did it start?

The creator of *The Archers*, Godfrey Baseley, devised the programme as a means of educating farmers in modern production methods when Britain was still subject to food rationing.

So it's an educational programme?

Not any more. *The Archers* lost its original educational remit in the early 1970s – but it still prides itself on the quality of its research and its reflection of real rural life.

How is it planned and written?

The Editor, Vanessa Whitburn, leads a ten-strong production team and nine or ten writers as they plot the complicated lives of the families in Ambridge, looking ahead months or sometimes years in biannual long-term meetings. The detailed planning is done at monthly script meetings about two months ahead of transmission. Each writer produces a week's worth of scripts in a remarkable 13 days.

... and recorded?

Actors receive their scripts a few days before recording, which takes place every four weeks in a state-of-the-art studio at the BBC's premises in the Mailbox complex in central Birmingham. Twenty-four episodes are recorded digitally in six intensive days, using only two hours of studio time per 13-minute episode. This schedule means that being an *Archers* actor is by no means a full time job, even for major characters, so many also have careers in film, theatre, television or other radio drama.

What's that 'dum-di-dum' tune?

The Archers' signature tune is a 'maypole dance': 'Barwick Green', from the suite *My Native Heath* by Yorkshire composer Arthur Wood.

How did you get that news item in?

Episodes are transmitted three to six weeks after recording. But listeners are occasionally intrigued to hear topical events reflected in that evening's broadcast, a feat achieved through a flurry of rewriting, re-recording and editing on the day of transmission.

CHARACTERS BY FORENAME

The characters in this book are listed alphabetically by surname or nickname. If you only know the forename, this should help you locate the relevant entry.

Adam Macy
Alan Franks
Alice Aldridge
Alistair Lloyd
Amy Franks
Baggy
Ben Archer
Bert Fry
Brenda Tucker
Brian Aldridge
Bunty and Reg Hebden
Caroline Sterling
Christine Barford
Christopher Carter
Clarrie Grundy
Clive Horrobin
Daniel Hebden Lloyd
David Archer
Debbie Aldridge
Derek Fletcher
Ed Grundy
Eddie Grundy
Edgar and Eileen Titcombe
Elizabeth Pargetter
Ellen Rogers
Emma Grundy
Fallon Rogers
Fat Paul
Freda Fry

George Grundy
Graham Ryder
Hayley Tucker
Hazel Woolley
Heather Pritchard
Helen Archer
Ian Craig
Jack Woolley
Jamie Perks
Jennifer Aldridge
Jill Archer
Joe Grundy
John Higgs
Jolene Perks
Josh Archer
Kate Madikane
Kathy Perks
Kenton Archer
Kirsty Miller
Lewis Carmichael
Lilian Bellamy
Lily and Freddie Pargetter
Lucas Madikane
Lynda Snell
Mandy and India Beesborough
Marjorie Antrobus
Matt Crawford
Maurice Horton
Mike Tucker

Neil Carter
Neville and Nathan Booth
Nic Hanson
Nigel Pargetter
Oliver Sterling
Owen King
Pat Archer
Peggy Woolley
Phil Archer
Phoebe Aldridge
Pip Archer
Rachel Dorsey
Robert Pullen
Robert Snell
Roy Tucker
Ruairi Donovan
Ruth Archer
Sabrina and Richard Thwaite
Satya Khanna
Shula Hebden Lloyd
Sid Perks
Snatch Foster
Stephen Chalkman
Susan Carter
Tom Archer
Tony Archer
Usha Gupta
Wayne Foley
William Grundy

Some can also be found under 'Silent Characters'

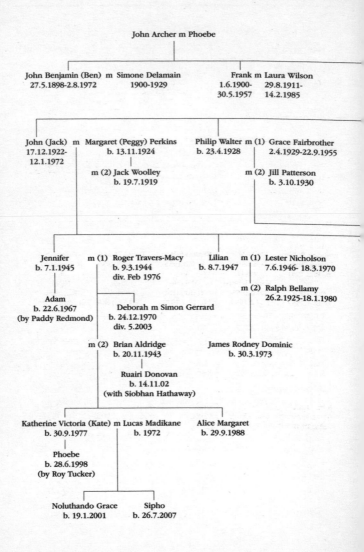

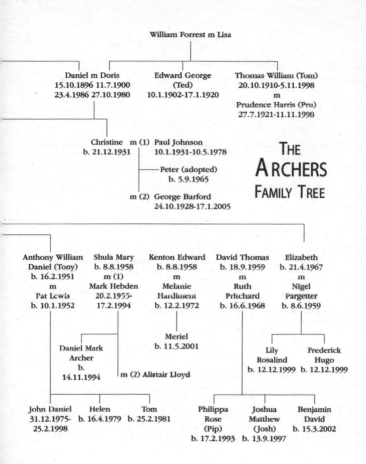

William Forrest m Lisa

Daniel m Doris
15.10.1896 11.7.1900
23.4.1986 27.10.1980

Edward George
(Ted)
10.1.1902-17.1.1920

Thomas William (Tom)
20.10.1910-5.11.1998
m
Prudence Harris (Pru)
27.7.1921-11.11.1998

Christine m (1) Paul Johnson
b. 21.12.1931   10.1.1931-10.5.1978

Peter (adopted)
b. 5.9.1965

m (2) George Barford
24.10.1928-17.1.2005

THE
ARCHERS
FAMILY TREE

Anthony William
Daniel (Tony)
b. 16.2.1951
m
Pat Lewis
b. 10.1.1952

Shula Mary
b. 8.8.1958
m (1)
Mark Hebden
20.2.1955-
17.2.1994

Kenton Edward
b. 8.8.1958
m
Melanie
Hardiment
b. 12.2.1972

David Thomas
b. 18.9.1959
m
Ruth
Pritchard
b. 16.6.1968

Elizabeth
b. 21.4.1967
m
Nigel
Pargetter
b. 8.6.1959

Daniel Mark
Archer
b.
14.11.1994

Meriel
b. 11.5.2001

m (2) Alistair Lloyd

Lily
Rosalind
b. 12.12.1999

Frederick
Hugo
b. 12.12.1999

John Daniel
31.12.1975-
25.2.1998

Helen
b. 16.4.1979

Tom
b. 25.2.1981

Philippa
Rose
(Pip)
b. 17.2.1993

Joshua
Matthew
(Josh)
b. 13.9.1997

Benjamin
David
b. 15.3.2002

ALICE ALDRIDGE

On a gap year in South Africa • Born 29.9.88

(Hollie Chapman)

In October 2007, Alice left **Home Farm** to start a gap year, helping her sister **Kate Madikane** at an AIDS project in Johannesburg. Having achieved excellent GCSE results, Alice had left her posh private school to study A level psychology, maths, design technology and physics at **Borchester** College. Despite her father **Brian**'s expectations of a nosedive in academic standards, she then attained similarly excellent A level grades. Alice reacted violently to the news that she had an illicit half-brother – **Ruairi Donovan** – and was unimpressed by her family's protests that they had kept the secret so as not to ruin her exams. And her decision to seek RAF sponsorship for her engineering degree didn't go down well with her friend **Amy Franks**.

BRIAN ALDRIDGE

Home Farm • Born 20.11.43
(Charles Collingwood)

Brian has sailed close to the wind in the past, but **Jennifer** always managed to forgive his extra-marital affairs, partly for the comfortable life this wealthy farmer has been able to give her. But when Brian's mistress Siobhan Hathaway (née Donovan) bore him **Ruairi Donovan** and then tragically died, leaving him to care for his son, the Aldridge marriage was assailed as never before. Brian's relationship with his other children suffered too: stepson **Adam Macy** and stepdaughter **Debbie** buried their personal differences as they fought for their place in the changed future of the farm, while daughter **Alice** had to recast her father's image in a much poorer light. **Kate**, more cynical and insulated by distance, was least affected both by the news of her new sibling and by his devastating arrival at **Home Farm**.

DEBBIE ALDRIDGE

(formerly Gerrard, née Travers-Macy)
Hungary • Born 24.12.70
(Tamsin Greig)

This human boomerang, the daughter of **Jennifer Aldridge** and her first husband, Roger Travers-Macy, has left home four times. She cut short her French degree because of an affair with lecturer Simon Gerrard, who later pursued and married her. But he turned out as much lecher as lecturer, and the marriage collapsed in 2002. Six months later, unable to accept **Brian**'s own extramarital affair, bruised Debbie fled **Home Farm** for a job in France. Her return in 2004 generated continued friction with half-brother **Adam Macy** over farm policy. In 2005, Debbie took a job running a farm in Hungary for a consortium including Brian, and the following year Adam was further irritated when **Matt Crawford** put her in charge of the **Estate** land. But the siblings united to protect their interests in 2007, when little **Ruairi Donovan** arrived on the scene.

JENNIFER ALDRIDGE

(formerly Travers-Macy, née Archer)
Home Farm • Born 7.1.45
(Angela Piper)

Elegant and a great cook, Jennifer loves being a mother and put her early career as a teacher and writer on hold to devote herself to her family. Pregnant by a local farmhand, unmarried Jennifer gave birth to **Adam** (now **Macy**) in 1967. She later married Roger Travers-Macy, who adopted Adam. They had a daughter, **Debbie**, but the marriage didn't last and Jennifer wed **Brian** in 1976. More daughters followed: **Kate** (now **Madikane**) and **Alice**, who left school when Jennifer was in her sixties. Jennifer thought she had finished her parenting and was looking forward to more grandmotherly times with Kate's daughter **Phoebe**. So you can imagine the torment she endured before agreeing to take Brian's illegitimate child **Ruairi Donovan** into her home. It's a tough woman who could take on that commitment. She's **Peggy Woolley**'s daughter, all right.

PHOEBE ALDRIDGE

Willow Farm • Born 28.6.98
(Scarlett Wakelin)

Who's the mummy? Well, it's not **Hayley Tucker**, despite appearances to the contrary. Phoebe is the product of a short-lived union between Hayley's husband **Roy** and **Kate Madikane**, who now lives in Johannesburg. With Kate in charge, Phoebe had the full hippy trappings: birth in a tepee at the Glastonbury Festival and a New Age naming ceremony on Lakey Hill. Her upbringing under Roy and Hayley's care has been rather more conventional.

AMBRIDGE

Picture a traditional English village. The image in your head is probably not a million miles from Ambridge. Village green with duck pond? Check. Village Hall? Check. Half-timbered pub? Check (**The Bull**). **Village Shop**? Check (thanks to **Jack Woolley**). Ludicrously priced thatched cottages, unsympathetic modern infill and early-morning departures by grey-faced commuters? Check, check and check. Gorgeous views and rubbish bus service? Checkity check. With all its 21st-century pressures, the English countryside still has a lot to offer. Just ask the folk in Ambridge if they'd prefer life in a city…

AMBRIDGE HALL

It could be argued that Ambridge Hall, with six bedrooms, is much too large for **Robert** and **Lynda Snell**, even with Scruff (**Daniel Hebden Lloyd**'s former dog) around the place. So when the IT industry no longer seemed to need Robert's services, Lynda suggested they might take in B&B guests. The place does have a lot to offer: attractive landscaped gardens, including a Shakespearean section – using only plants named by the Bard – and a low allergen area, to which Lynda retreats when her annual hay fever descends. But the *pièce de résistance* is in the paddock. How many guest houses could boast a trio of llamas, after all?

AMBRIDGE ORGANICS

Not a 'farm shop' exactly, as they are usually on the farm itself, but the 'farm's shop' – **Bridge Farm**'s, that is. Ambridge Organics is owned by **Pat** and **Tony Archer** and managed by their daughter **Helen**, employing **silent** Anya and **Kirsty Miller**, former girlfriend of Helen's brother **Tom**. The shop provides an ethical alternative to **Underwoods**' food hall, selling Bridge Farm veg, yoghurt and ice-cream, plus a whole range of bought-in organic produce.

MARJORIE ANTROBUS

The Laurels • Born 1922
(Margot Boyd)

The Laurels nursing home looks to be the penultimate destination for this much-travelled lady, once a mainstay of **St Stephen's Church** and **Ambridge** parish council. Marjorie has memories aplenty to share with her visitors of her time as a colonial wife in Kenya and elsewhere, and later as a leading breeder of Afghan hounds.

BEN ARCHER

Brookfield Farm • Born 15.3.02

(Thomas Lester)

Although they are used to breeding replacement heifers for the dairy herd, **David** and **Ruth** had to assure **Josh** that the same principle didn't apply when they produced a younger sibling. Anyway, the new one turned out to be male, so would have been a rubbish milker. Dark-haired and lively, Ben started at Loxley Barrett Primary in 2006.

DAVID ARCHER

Brookfield Farm • Born 18.9.59
(Timothy Bentinck)

Husband to **Ruth**, devoted father to **Pip**, **Josh** and **Ben**, stalwart of the **Ambridge** cricket team and a parish councillor. Having taken on **Brookfield Farm** in 2001 (much to the disgruntlement of squabbling siblings **Elizabeth Pargetter** and **Kenton**), it seemed like a good idea to recruit specialist herdsman Sam Batton to maximise the revenue from their expanded dairy herd. But in 2006 David's former fiancée Sophie Barlow reappeared with an adulterous agenda. David spurned her advances too late to stop unhappy Ruth nearly sleeping with Sam. With both third parties off the scene, David worked hard to rebuild his marriage but found that trust, once broken, was a very fragile thing.

HELEN ARCHER

Bridge Farm • Born 16.4.79
(Louiza Patikas)

Two bereavements have caused **Pat** and **Tony Archer**'s daughter continuing psychological problems. Her elder brother John died in an accident in 1998, and her partner Greg Turner took his own life in 2004. Driven Helen's attempts to control her unhappy life led to anorexia and, in 2006, to uncontrolled drinking and partying. Time at a specialist clinic helped her recover from the former. Counselling – plus the shock of injuring **Mike Tucker** while driving over the limit – helped her understand and control the latter. With greater equilibrium, she returned to her busy life, drawing on her HND in food technology to manufacture **Borsetshire** Blue cheese and managing the farm's shop, **Ambridge Organics**.

JILL ARCHER

(née Patterson)
Glebe Cottage • Born 3.10.30
(Patricia Greene)

Seeing her with husband **Phil**, the casual observer might easily pop Jill into the pigeonhole marked 'farmer's wife (retired)'. Over 40 years, she's done much to merit that label, raising **Kenton**, **Shula** (now **Hebden Lloyd**), **David** and **Elizabeth** (now **Pargetter**) while helping with village life and on the farm – in fact she still tends **Brookfield**'s bees and hens. But there's more to the woman than these traditional values. Jill's radical streak is seen in her opposition to hunting and to private education, and in a more recent campaign to rid the local school of junk food.

JOSH ARCHER

Brookfield Farm • Born 13.9.97
(George Bingham)

Like many small boys, **David** and **Ruth**'s middle child has occasional wild enthusiasms. Previously attached to a charming plaything called a Killer Borg, in 2006 Josh took pity on an abandoned muntjac deer. Against their better judgement, his parents succumbed to Josh's piteous pestering and for a while the lad did keep his promise to look after 'Monty', even sharing his bed with him, to **Bert Fry**'s considerable disapproval. But eventually the novelty faded, so the beast was found a new home at **Lower Loxley Hall**. Monty, that is; not Josh.

KENTON ARCHER

April Cottage • Born 8.8.58
(Richard Attlee)

Kenton sees himself as a bon viveur and wit. Others would say he's more bonkers and a twit. But in recent years he's managed to defy his previous failures in business (having been bailed out by parents **Phil** and **Jill** at least twice) and has successfully held down a job as manager of **Jaxx Caff**. In 2007, he moved in with girlfriend **Kathy Perks** and makes a wonderful 'uncle' to her son **Jamie**. In fact, being an uncle is probably what he does best, and he's very popular with the Archer children, if not always with their parents. Kenton also has a daughter, Meriel, who lives in New Zealand. According to his ex-wife Mel, this is only just far enough away.

PAT ARCHER

(née Lewis)
Bridge Farm • Born 10.1.52
(Patricia Gallimore)

Pat and **Tony** were pioneers of the modern organic movement, eschewing chemicals at **Bridge Farm** as far back as 1984, but Pat's generally seen as the more go-ahead of the two – even by Tony. Her main responsibility is processing the farm's milk into yoghurt and ice-cream. But in 2006, fed up with Tony moaning about how many of his carrots were failing to meet the supermarkets' stringent size restrictions, she took the initiative and started to market them in the farm's own specially printed packaging. Even doubting Tony was eventually won over by the project, proof that Pat's ardour for supplying high quality food was unabated. If only the problems of her children **Tom** and – especially – **Helen** could be bagged up so easily.

PHIL ARCHER

Glebe Cottage • Born 23.4.28

(Norman Painting)

The 23rd of April is associated with three icons of England: Shakespeare, St George and Phil Archer. Through the 1960s and 1970s, Phil built up **Brookfield Farm**, finally passing it to son **David** and daughter-in-law **Ruth** in 2001. He's a staunch churchgoer – in fact, he's the church organist – and his marriage to **Jill** has been one of the most stable relationships in the village. In his retirement, Phil is very active, looking after Brookfield's previously neglected garden as well as his own; and his piano playing is always in demand for village productions. Although he sometimes overestimates the musical talents of his granddaughter **Pip**, in all other respects most reckon Phil to be an admirable man – despite an absence of playwriting or dragon slaying.

PIP ARCHER

Brookfield Farm • Born 17.2.93
(Helen Monks)

Like many teenagers, Pip has multiple personalities. At times she's a delight, particularly when she's taking an interest in the cows. But she's also reached the age that parents wish could be fast-forwarded, when the simplest request can be met with stentorian huffing and vertebrae-threatening head tossing. **Ruth** and **David** are resigned to toughing it out. As can often be the case at this tricky time, Pip sometimes gets on better with grandfather **Phil**, especially as she has inherited some of his musical talent. As well as playing the piano and clarinet, Pip sings in the choir at **Borchester** Green School with her friend **Izzy**.

RUTH ARCHER

(née Pritchard)
Brookfield Farm • Born 16.6.68
(Felicity Finch)

Ruth has been a fixture at **Brookfield** since she arrived from Prudoe in Northumberland in 1987, first as an agricultural student and then as **David**'s wife. She was forced to take a progressively less hands-on role on the farm following the welcome arrival of **Pip**, **Josh** and **Ben** and, in 2000, the absolutely unwelcome arrival of breast cancer. In 2006, she started to redress the balance, insisting that David become more acquainted with the dishwasher and the kids' homework timetables. But this brought her into ever-closer contact with Brookfield herdsman Sam Batton, who (rather inconveniently) adored her. Despite strong temptation, she did not sleep with Sam, but the marriage took a severe blow and the damaged trust caused David to worry what motivated Ruth's subsequent desire for a breast reconstruction, seven years after her mastectomy.

TOM ARCHER

The Nest, Home Farm • Born 25.2.81
(Tom Graham)

Ambitious Tom has had a few setbacks in his journey to become the sausage king of **Borsetshire**. It was only the intervention in 2005 of his hard-nosed uncle **Brian Aldridge** which saved Tom's over-extended pork business, and the uneasy relationship has caused friction with Tom's more idealistic parents **Pat** and **Tony**. But at least things went from strength to strength with Tom's girlfriend **Brenda Tucker** (sister of his friend **Roy**) and they moved in together in 2007. With a mobile catering business – Tom Archer's Gourmet Grills – helping to publicise his products and an increasing ability to hold his ground with Brian, Tom proved that what doesn't kill you makes you stronger.

TONY ARCHER

Bridge Farm • Born 16.2.51
(Colin Skipp)

Tony faces the unrelenting daily round of milking and the punishing demands of year-round veg production with a resigned weariness. The signs of age? No, he's been like that most of his adult life. He keeps plugging away, committed – like wife **Pat** – to the organic cause and trying not to think of the plush lives of his sisters **Jennifer Aldridge** and **Lilian Bellamy**. Tony can be cheered up occasionally. A pint of Shires helps, as does a summer drive in his classic MG Midget. But not in combination. That's what got daughter **Helen** into so much trouble.

ARKWRIGHT HALL

If you are looking for some interesting self-catering accommodation in **Ambridge**, could we suggest Arkwright Hall? This large Victorian house with a 17th-century core was once a community centre 'with soundproofed room for rock and roll' and later a field studies centre but it remained unoccupied and unloved for a long time. Architect **Lewis Carmichael** supervised the building's restoration to its Victorian splendour and the owner **Jack Woolley** leased it to the Landmark Trust. As housekeeper, **Freda Fry** cleans the place between lets.

BAGGY

Borchester

Baggy, **Snatch Foster** and **Eddie Grundy** were once the Freeman, Hardy and Willis of **Borsetshire**; they always had something afoot. Although (unlike those celebrated shoe-sellers) it was usually something dodgy. But Snatch took it a dodge too far with his illegal meat scam, so Baggy is now Eddie's main accomplice, often helping with the spectrum of Grundy activities, from laying patios to poaching.

CHRISTINE BARFORD

(formerly Johnson, née Archer)
Woodbine Cottage • Born 21.12.31
(Lesley Saweard)

Phil **Archer**'s younger sister Chris – as she's always known in the family – lives a quiet retirement after many years running a riding stable (now owned by her niece **Shula Hebden Lloyd**) and two very different marriages. Peter, her adopted son from her first marriage, travels a lot as an administrator with a symphony orchestra. After the death of Peter's flaky father, Paul Johnson, Chris found more secure happiness with solid, dependable George Barford. But sadly George died in 2005 while they were waiting to reoccupy their house after a horrific firebomb attack. Arsonist **Clive Horrobin** was targeting his long-time enemy, gamekeeper and former policeman George. He was sentenced to 12 years, but that wasn't much comfort to Chris, who faced her declining years as a widow once again.

MANDY AND INDIA BEESBOROUGH

Mandy Born 1953
(Loxley Barratt)

Mandy, the red-haired, vivacious doyenne of the Pony Club, has produced a similarly luscious and horsey daughter. India Beesborough is a friend and former schoolmate of **Alice Aldridge**. **Susan Carter** nurses the hope that her son **Christopher** might hook up with India one day. **Jennifer Aldridge** nurses the hope that her husband **Brian** doesn't hook up (again, it's rumoured) with Mandy.

LILIAN BELLAMY

(formerly Nicholson, née Archer)
The Dower House • Born 8.7.47
(Sunny Ormonde)

After many louche years as a tax exile in Guernsey following the death of her second husband Ralph, Lilian returned to **Ambridge**, apparently with the intention of teaching her siblings **Jennifer Aldridge** and **Tony Archer** the true meaning of the word 'embarrassment'. Lilian has certainly ignored the adage 'never go back'. In 2006, she bought a majority share in **The Bull**, the pub in which she'd grown up, and moved back into the home she'd once shared with Ralph. This time it was with her 'Tiger', **Matt Crawford**, who seems to delight in pushing the boundaries of the relationship. Most people think they deserve each other. Lilian's son James (born in 1973) paid her a rare visit in 2005, but sadly his only objective was getting a shed-load of money to shore up an overambitious property deal.

NEVILLE AND NATHAN BOOTH

Neville Born 1942
Ambridge

Neville is a bell-ringer at **St Stephen's**, but of late his nephew Nathan has been making more of a noise in **Ambridge**. Once disqualified from a nettle-eating contest at **The Bull** (for numbing his mouth with ice cubes), slimy Nathan was beaten by **Lilian Bellamy** and (narrowly) **Lynda Snell** for election to Ambridge parish council in 2006. He contents himself with membership – in partnership with **Graham Ryder** – of the world's smallest pub quiz team. The Straighten Arrows are similar to Millwall Football Club, at least in their defiant attitude: 'everyone hates us, we don't care'.

BORCHESTER

This market town lies in the picturesque Am Vale six miles north-east of **Ambridge**. At its heart is a historic clock tower and wool market. Pubs and hotels include the comfortable George, the Tin of Peaches (near the canning factory) and the Goat and Nightgown (very lively thanks to its proximity to Borchester General Hospital and Borchester College). There's a good range of shops, including **Underwoods** department store and **Ambridge Organics**. Leisure facilities include the Theatre Royal, a three-screen cinema and a municipal leisure centre with gym and swimming pool. Cafés and restaurants range from **Jaxx Caff** to the upmarket Botticelli's, plus the usual range of ethnic establishments and takeaways.

BORCHESTER LAND

No one is quite sure what attracted the attention of this aggressive property company to the **Ambridge** area, but a lot of locals wish it had had grit in its eye at the time. BL owns the 1,020-acre Berrow **Estate**, which includes business units at Sawyer's Farm and the tenanted **Bridge Farm**. In 2003, it converted a few acres of agricultural land for an ill-received luxury housing development, **Grange Spinney**. All this was under the lairy chairmanship of **Matt Crawford**. Matt enjoys the business opportunities afforded by the Estate's extensive pheasant shoot, in which fellow director **Brian Aldridge** plays a large part. As Brian is the *acceptable* face of Borchester Land, you'll understand that Matt is to the countryside what Wayne Rooney is to needlepoint.

BORSETSHIRE

Some people say they have trouble finding Borsetshire on the map. They obviously aren't looking hard enough. Stare in the right frame of mind at the borders of Worcestershire and Warwickshire to the south-west of Birmingham and you will discover a charming, predominantly rural county, dominated to the east by the cathedral city and administrative centre of **Felpersham**. The second-largest settlement is the market town of **Borchester**. **Ambridge** lies south-east of the Hassett Hills and falls under South Borsetshire District Council. The main local newspapers are the *Felpersham Advertiser*, the *Westbury Courier* and the *Borchester Echo*, and the area is served by Radio Borsetshire. Right, now let's look for Narnia...

BRIDGE FARM

STOCK
95 milkers (Friesians) • 46 followers (heifers/calves)

CROPS
115 acres grassland • 20 acres barley
15 acres wheat • 6 acres potatoes
4 acres carrots • 2 acres leeks
3 acres swedes • 2 acres Dutch cabbage
1 acre Savoy cabbage
4 acres mixed vegetable and salad crops,
including two polytunnels

LABOUR
Tony Archer • **Pat Archer** • **Tom Archer**
Clarrie Grundy (dairy) • Colin Kennedy (dairy)

Tenant farmers **Tony** and **Pat Archer** rent 140 acres from the **Estate**, with an extra 32 acres from other landlords. Bridge Farm converted to organic in 1984. The farm's produce – including yoghurt and ice-cream made in their own dairy – is sold through a wholesaler and to local outlets including **Ambridge Organics**. In 2005, ambitious **Tom**'s sausage business collapsed, forcing him to start again under the control of his uncle **Brian Aldridge**.

BROOKFIELD FARM

STOCK

190 milkers (Friesians) • 85 followers (heifers/calves)
85 beef cattle (Herefords) • 340 ewes
Hens (small scale) • 337 acres grassland
70 acres cereals • 10 acres oilseed rape
15 acres potatoes • 12 acres beans
17 acres forage maize
8 acres set-aside

LABOUR

David Archer (managing)
Ruth Archer (managing and herdsperson)
Eddie Grundy (relief herdsperson)
Bert Fry (retired, casual)
Biff (sheepdog)

Brookfield is a 469-acre mixed farm incorporating the old holdings of Marney's and Hollowtree. After **Phil**'s retirement in 2001, **David** and **Ruth** contracted out the arable work to **Home Farm** and expanded the dairy herd. Brookfield is doing its best to move away from selling its products as commodities and to get closer to the customer. High-quality beef from the Herefords is sold at the farm gate, and the lamb is marketed co-operatively under the Hassett Hills brand.

THE BULL

Location: **Ambridge**, *near village green*
Appearance: Half-timbered, chocolate box
Outside facilities: Car park, beer garden,
    boules piste, resident peacock (Eccles?!)
Bars: Public, lounge ('Ploughmans')
Food: Bar snacks and family restaurant
Beer: Shires, very well kept
Other facilities: Skittles, darts, two computers
    – internet access, upstairs function room
Entertainment: music nights, quizzes
Management: Free house. **Sid Perks** *(a bit old*
    school), **Jolene Perks** *– wow! Part owner*
    Lilian Bellamy

Inspector's notes from South Borsetshire Pub of the Year
competition.

LEWIS CARMICHAEL

Lower Loxley Hall
(Robert Lister)

Charming Lewis officially retired as an architect but still does the occasional job that interests him, like the conversion of **Lower Loxley**'s shop and café, the refurbishment of **Arkwright Hall** or the extension of buildings at The Stables to form **Alistair Lloyd**'s veterinary surgery. He also agreed to serve on the committee trying to revitalise the old Cat and Fiddle pub, until it was instead redeveloped as flats. These occasional tasks left him plenty of time to woo **Nigel Pargetter**'s mother, Julia. They were married on 26 May 2005, but sadly their happiness was short-lived, as Julia died six months later. He still runs Lower Loxley's art gallery.

CHRISTOPHER CARTER

Ambridge View • Born 22.6.88
(William Sanderson-Thwaite)

Like his father **Neil**, Chris is a keen cricketer and a bell-ringer. He sounded the death knell for **Susan**'s hopes that at least one Carter would gain a degree when he announced in 2004 that he wanted to pursue a career as a farrier. But Neil was delighted when **Ronnie** took his son on. Chris buckled down to the four-year training scheme, and his developing musculature made him a popular visitor to the area's stables and riding schools. Susan at least hoped that Chris would make the most of the social opportunities offered by close proximity to the horse-owning classes. Indeed, he has had at least one very posh girlfriend, the Lord Lieutenant's niece, Venetia Streatfield. But he dumped her to go out with a part-time barmaid from the wrong end of **Borchester**. Sorry, Susan…

NEIL CARTER

Ambridge View • Born 22.5.57
(Brian Hewlett)

Don't mention former employer **Tom Archer** to Neil or his wife **Susan**, as they still feel he let them down badly when his business had to retrench in 2005. Neil and Susan live in a self-built house on Neil's eight acres at **Willow Farm**. If that sounds a lot of land, you have to remember that it's shared by Neil's outdoor herd of Gloucester Old Spot pigs and the free-range hens which he runs with **Hayley Tucker**. Actually, don't mention the Grundy family either, as daughter **Emma** married **Will Grundy**, had his child **George**, rejected Will for **Ed**, divorced Will and then became estranged from Ed too. Hell's bells, as Neil might have said (after all, he is the tower captain at **St Stephen's**).

SUSAN CARTER

(née Horrobin)
Ambridge View • Born 10.10.63
(Charlotte Martin)

The high-flyers among us might think that managing the **Village Shop** and post office isn't much to write home about. But when that home was originally 6, The Green – the chaotic headquarters of the infamous **Horrobin** family – it's actually quite a step up. Susan's climb to respectability has been a rocky one. She even went to prison in 1993 when forced to shelter her fugitive criminal brother **Clive**. She has had to accept that husband **Neil** will always be a pigman, and is realising that son **Christopher** might have a good career ahead of him as a farrier. But Susan dearly wishes that **Emma** (now **Grundy**) could move on from her low-grade jobs and difficult love life. Susan likes to be the gossiper, not the gossipee.

CASA NUEVA

The gamekeeper's tied cottage at **Home Farm** is in quite an isolated spot, on a lane bordering Lyttleton Covert. It's not been the happiest of homes in recent years. The previous occupant – **Will Grundy**'s former head keeper Greg Turner – committed suicide while living there. At least he had the grace not to blight the place totally, committing the deed nearby rather than actually in the cottage. Will and **Emma Grundy** christened the place 'new house' in Spanish, in memory of their Mexican honeymoon, and spent the first few months of their ill-starred marriage there. When Emma left, Will remained in bitter defiance with his dogs Meg and Mitch, and did his best to make it a cheerful home on the days their son **George** spent with him. The arrival of Will's new girlfriend **Nic Hanson** and her two children made a big difference.

STEPHEN CHALKMAN

Borchester
(David Kendall)

Long-term associate of **Matt Crawford**. When 'Chalky' was a member of South Borsetshire District Council's planning committee, he forgot to mention that his wife Mererid Calder was a director of **Borchester Land**'s parent company. Embarrassing that, when the council was considering a Borchester Land application for what eventually became **Grange Spinney**. When Matt was trying to hide money during his divorce, he 'paid' Chalkman a large sum as Matt's 'financial consultant'. Matt also 'lost' £50,000 to his old mate in a very well-staged poker game, complete with upstanding landowner **Nigel Pargetter** as a witness. In 2005, the partners in, er, business invested in the conversion of the old Cat and Fiddle pub to luxury flats, to **Lynda Snell**'s disgust.

IAN CRAIG

Honeysuckle Cottage • Born 1970
(Stephen Kennedy)

Although easy-going socially, the head chef at **Grey Gables** is a stickler at work and is a big part of the hotel's continuing success. Much to the discomfiture of **Sid Perks** and certain other residents, this affable Northern Irelander and his partner **Adam Macy** occupy a cottage prominently located on the village green. Their generally stable relationship was rocked when Ian's old friend Madeleine (Madds) asked him to father a child with her. It caused huge conflict with reluctant Adam – and then mercurial Madds found a more conventional possible father. But Ian and Adam emerged from all the angst with a strengthened relationship and were 'married' in a civil partnership in December 2006. It raised another problem for Ian, though, who had to come out to his traditional Ulster farming family. Despite **Brian Aldridge**'s unease, Ian became a wonderul extra uncle to **Ruairi Donovan**.

MATT CRAWFORD

The Dower House
(Kim Durham)

After a messy and expensive divorce from Yvette, Matt shacked up with lover **Lilian Bellamy** and in 2006 they bought Lilian's former home, the **Dower House**. As this is the poshest residence in **Ambridge**, you'll understand that Matt isn't short of 50p for the gas meter. A Londoner, ambitious Matt started in sales and climbed the greasy pole to become chairman of **Borchester Land** and the driving force behind its dominance of the Ambridge property scene. He despises the **Grundys**, but ironically they have much in common, notably a flexible approach to any legislation which might hamper their business dealings.

RUAIRI DONOVAN

Home Farm • Born 14.11.02
(Matthew Rocket)

Illegitimate (quaint word nowadays, we know) product of an extramarital affair between **Brian Aldridge** and the deceased Siobhan Hathaway (née Donovan). When Brian made the choice to stay with **Jennifer** rather than starting a new life with Siobhan, he imagined that his relationship with Ruairi (pronounced 'Rory') would be tenuous at best, especially when Siobhan moved to Germany. But her death from cancer in May 2007 brought the boy – after mighty ructions – to **Home Farm**. Brian and Jennifer struggled to integrate the poor, lost child into their family, knowing that it was just the start of an extraordinarily difficult road.

RACHEL DORSEY

Felpersham

Rachel arrived as archdeacon of **Felpersham** diocese in 2007. She was very supportive of the relationship between **Ambridge**'s vicar **Alan Franks** and **Usha Gupta**. Rachel and Alan had a similar, modernising outlook and soon embarked on several radical projects, to the consternation of some of the more traditional parishioners.

THE DOWER HOUSE

*'... This fine res, historically the home of the squires of **Ambridge**, benefits from lg ent hl, din rm, sttg rm, stdy, 2 frthr recp rms, wl appntd kit, lndry, 6 bdrms, 3 with en suite, sep offc suite. Lg gdn, lawns and stbls, superb views...'* (That's enough estate agent speak. Ed.) **Lilian** and Ralph **Bellamy** lived here in the 1970s. More recently, it was home to **Caroline Sterling**, who sold it in 2006 to fund the purchase of **Grey Gables**. To whom did she sell it? Why, **Matt Crawford**, now the partner of the same Lilian Bellamy.

THE ESTATE

More correctly, the Berrow Estate: see **Borchester Land**.

FAT PAUL

There are quite a few Fat Pauls around. One is a DJ, another a guitarist in a punk band. Our Fat Paul – building contractor Paul Blocker – has musically related talents too. Sort of. He managed to squeeze himself into the cab of his JCB to perform a comically awful 'Disco Diggers' routine with friend **Eddie Grundy** at the 2001 **Ambridge** fete. But even more memorable than that is his party piece, which involves the shedding of his size XXXL clothes to the strains of *Agadoo* – and a high incidence of post-traumatic stress disorder among any unfortunate witnesses.

FELPERSHAM

This cathedral city, the county town of **Borsetshire**, stands 17 miles east of **Ambridge**. With an extensive shopping centre, cafés, eating places and nightspots, it entertains many a credit card-crazed consumer who can't be bothered to travel the extra distance to Birmingham.

DEREK FLETCHER

Glebelands

For many years, **Ambridge** parish council was under the popular chairmanship first of **Jack Woolley** and then of **Christine Barford**'s husband George. Then on George's death came... Derek Fletcher. More 'little England' than 'middle England', Derek and Pat occupy a gnome-encircled 'executive home' in Glebelands – the **Grange Spinney** of its day. Along with **Peggy Woolley**, Derek was one of the parishioners unable to accept a woman vicar at **St Stephen's** and has been known to send anonymous poison pen letters, too. He is still trying to get over the arrival in the village of **Usha Gupta** – and that happened in 1991.

WAYNE FOLEY

Radio Borsetshire
(Ian Brooker)

A former colleague of **Brenda Tucker**, before she decided to improve her chances by going to university, Wayne presents the afternoon show on Radio **Borsetshire**. He's a big fish in a small pond, as **Brian Aldridge** once said. Well, it sounded like 'total carp', anyway…

SNATCH FOSTER

Borchester

While not totally law-abiding, the **Grundys** at least have their own moral code, one of the principal injunctions being 'you don't stitch up a mate'. Not so the Fosters. Snatch once supplied **Eddie Grundy** with meat 'from a hill farmer doing a bit of slaughtering'. Eddie sold cuts (illegally but, he thought, not dangerously) at car-boot sales. The meat was actually condemned. Eddie was fined heavily and was lucky to escape jail. Snatch went down for two years. By a strange turn of fate, Eddie's godson – Snatch's boy Bruno – turned up in the village under the foster care of **Oliver** and **Caroline Sterling**. Bruno tried to take revenge for Eddie grassing Snatch up – until he discovered the full story of his father's duplicity.

ALAN FRANKS

The Vicarage
(John Telfer)

Alan isn't afraid to flout convention, which in a traditional rural community has made him a sometimes controversial figure. A former accountant who worked as a non-stipendiary minister in Nottingham, Alan was appointed vicar of **Ambridge**, Penny Hassett, Darrington and Edgeley in June 2003. Activities which have kept the local gossips busy have included tearing up the lanes on his motorbike (often in the company of Hindu girlfriend **Usha Gupta**), abseiling down the church tower and taking a young heroin addict into his home. This last was thought particularly unwise, given the presence of his daughter **Amy**, who protested that she could look after herself, thanks. Alan's wife Catherine (who was black) died of breast cancer in 1995. Despite their close bond, Amy was pleased when her father found new love with Usha.

AMY FRANKS

The Vicarage • Born 1989
(Vinette Robinson)

There are feisty genes on both sides of Amy's family. Her father **Alan** isn't afraid of a fight and nor is his mother-in-law Mabel (Amy's mother is dead). Mabel, originally from Jamaica but a long-term resident of Bradford, visits occasionally, bringing a bunch of strong opinions in tow. Amy took her A levels in 2007, intending to qualify as a midwife. She has radical views and is often on Alan's case over environmental matters, so it's no surprise that her friendship with **Alice Aldridge** was severely tested by Alice's involvement in foxhunting and more recently by Alice's plans for a career with the RAF.

BERT FRY

Brookfield Bungalow • Born 1936

(Eric Allan)

We will sing of Bert Fry, gardener
*Spouse of **Freda**, Trevor's father*
*Tills the soil at **Brookfield** stoutly*
Choosing not a full retirement
Working on a casual basis.
Warden at the church of Stephen
Umpire for the village cricket
Well known he for repetition
Of his stories old and rural.
Why, you ask, this versifying?
Bert Fry is a bard of Borset
Versifies to all and sundry
With his many poems. Plural.

Brookfield Bungalow

The Fry marriage has been a traditional one. Freda doesn't just cook and clean at home; she's the mainstay of **The Bull**'s kitchen and is the housekeeper at **Arkwright Hall**. She and **Bert** celebrated their golden wedding anniversary in 2006 with an unusually adventurous trip to India. Only the most unreconstructed would attribute the longevity of the relationship to the fact that Freda is never heard to speak.

GRANGE FARM

STOCK
30 milkers (Guernseys)

CROPS
50 acres grassland

LABOUR
Oliver Sterling (managing and relief) • **Ed Grundy**
(herd manager) • **Mike Tucker** (dairy)

A working farm – although some may dispute that description – until the bankrupt **Grundys** were evicted in 2000. The bulk of the acreage was absorbed back into the **Estate** and the farmhouse sold with 50 acres to **Oliver Sterling**. In 2006 Oliver replaced his beef cattle with a small herd of Guernseys to supply **Mike Tucker**'s milk round. Confounding the sceptics, it provided a full-time job for **Ed Grundy** and an important new challenge for bereaved Mike, who did much of the on-farm processing and bottling. And 2007 saw the launch of Sterling Gold, an unpasteurised cheese.

GRANGE SPINNEY

If **Matt Crawford** had his way, **Ambridge** would rival Birmingham for urban sprawl. This **Borchester Land** development of 12 luxury houses and six 'low cost' homes, built in 2003, is a step on the way.

GREY GABLES

After a refurbishment in 2004, with excellent facilities including a health club and golf course, and with go-ahead chef **Ian Craig** aiming for his first Michelin star, Grey Gables became a hotel fit for the 21st century. So when it was put on the market as owner **Jack Woolley**'s mental powers failed, it made an attractive business proposition. Manager **Caroline Sterling** sold all she had and with the support of husband **Oliver** – and the bank – made a successful bid in 2006. **Roy Tucker**'s subsequent promotion to deputy manager upset **Lynda Snell** more than somewhat but her elevation to 'senior' receptionist did a little to reduce her umbridge. No: *'umbridge'*.

CLARRIE GRUNDY

Keeper's Cottage • Born 12.5.54
(Rosalind Adams)

Behind every good man there's a good woman, goes the old saying. To **Eddie**'s credit, he once said that Clarrie wasn't behind him; she'd always been beside him. And Clarrie is a very good woman, even if her husband rarely fits that description. Clarrie works incessantly, cooking and cleaning for Eddie, curmudgeonly father-in-law **Joe** and son **Ed**, whom she is forever trying to reconcile with elder son **William**. And she holds down two jobs, in the dairy at **Bridge Farm** and behind the bar at **The Bull**. To escape her daily drudgery, Clarrie likes a nice romantic novel (not that she gets much time to read) and very occasionally escapes to Great Yarmouth to see her sister, Rosie Mabbott. But her best ever holidays have been very occasional trips to her beloved France.

ED GRUNDY

Keeper's Cottage • Born 28.9.84

(Barry Farrimond)

Few would have put money on Ed becoming a model employee, as herd manager at **Grange Farm**. He's served community punishments for joyriding and burglary and in 2004 he tried to grow cannabis in a barn at **Bridge Farm** with his mate **Jazzer**. Ed sensed a chance of salvation when **Emma Grundy** and Ed's beloved nephew **George** moved in with him, prior to Emma's divorce from his brother **William**. But in 2006 the strains of the difficult relationship were too much for Emma, who moved back with her parents. Ed went AWOL in a miasma of drink and drugs, to the despair of parents **Eddie** and **Clarrie**. But with the support of his employer and patron **Oliver Sterling**, and a platonic friendship with **Fallon Rogers**, Ed eventually found a way of living with his hurt.

EDDIE GRUNDY

Keeper's Cottage • Born 15.3.51
(Trevor Harrison)

Eddie works in all shades of the economy, from legitimate casual work on the farms of **Ambridge** – often using his ancient tractor or digger – to a variety of other enterprises, some not even guessed at by the taxman. He's your man for garden ornaments, compost, landscaping, dodgy meat... OK, he admits that last one was a bit of a mistake. With his father **Joe**, Eddie was the tenant of **Grange Farm** before they went bust in 2000. He long ago shelved his hopes of making it big as a country and western singer and now contents himself with being master of **Grundys' Field**.

EMMA GRUNDY

(née Carter)
Ambridge View • Born 7.8.84
(Felicity Jones)

This is the life of Emma Grundy... Disappointing GCSE results. Disappointed her mother **Susan Carter** by taking a job as assistant manager of **Jaxx Caff**. Disappointed her father **Neil** when pregnant by **Will Grundy**. Disappointed **Ed Grundy** by marrying Will. Disappointed Will by believing baby **George** was Ed's. Disappointed Will (and Neil and Susan) by leaving Will for Ed. Disappointed Ed when George wasn't his. Disappointed **Kenton Archer** for messing him around over her maternity leave. Disappointed herself over conflict with Will about George. Disappointed Ed by moving back in with Neil and Susan. Disappointed **Eddie** and **Clarrie Grundy** for devastating the lives of their two sons. Disappointed when Will started dating again.

Disappointing, isn't it?

GEORGE GRUNDY

Ambridge View / Casa Nueva • Born 7.4.05

This little chap fitted more familial complications into his first year than many people have in their whole lives. He was named George after **William Grundy**'s former gamekeeping mentor George Barford and Edward after... well, who? Grandfather **Eddie**? Or Will's brother **Ed**, whom **Emma** mistakenly believed to be George's real father? A DNA test proved otherwise. Not much later Emma was divorced from Will and estranged from Ed. Although resident with his mum, George spends regular days and nights with Will. His parents managed to put the split behind them and move on, for George's benefit. Not so Uncle Ed, whose plans of a future with Emma and George crashed and burned.

JOE GRUNDY

Keeper's Cottage • Born 18.9.21
(Edward Kelsey)

Joe's always been prepared to share everything he has with you, but unfortunately he's never had anything, or at least that's his story. Although he still feels the odium of being the Grundy who lost the tenancy of **Grange Farm** (through bankruptcy), the purchase of **Grundys' Field** brightened his 80th year. And he's been cheered by seeing grandson **Ed** in a responsible position at their old home under its new owner **Oliver Sterling**. Thanks to his trap, with pony Bartleby, Joe keeps as mobile as he wants, which is mainly between home and sources of decent cider, including his own potent farmhouse brew. He tends the gardens at Keeper's Cottage and neighbouring April Cottage and provides a constant source of outrage for **Lynda Snell** across the road. He thinks of it as a public service.

WILLIAM GRUNDY

Casa Nueva • Born 9.2.83
(Philip Molloy)

Clarrie and **Eddie**'s elder son has the well-connected **Caroline Sterling** as godmother. After the death of Greg Turner, **Brian Aldridge** was persuaded to promote Will to head keeper at the combined **Grey Gables**, Berrow **Estate** and **Home Farm** shoot, with a tied cottage to boot. This was topped off in 2004 by his marriage to the lovely **Emma** Carter and the arrival a few months later of their son **George**. But, oh, how things changed when Emma left Will for his hated brother **Ed**. A bitter divorce followed and it was a long time before arrangements for George's mutual care could be described as amicable. But things started to look up in 2007. Will received a substantial inheritance from a distant aunt and started his first relationship since the divorce, with older mother-of-two **Nic Hanson**

GRUNDYS' FIELD

Given their 'druthers', the **Grundys** would rather be farming their old tenanted holding **Grange Farm** but since their bankruptcy in 2000 this 3.4 acres will have to do. At least they own this patch of land, and have been pretty creative in turning it to economic advantage. In the colder months they raise Christmas turkeys and over-winter sheep for hill farmers. Spring and summer see car-boot sales, with children entertained by the Berkshire sow Barbarella. A pole barn houses **Eddie**'s ancient tractor and digger, and in a rough shed and (shudder, **Lynda Snell**) an old shipping container he stores his stock-in-trade: garden ornaments and materials for his landscaping business. The picture is completed with delightful mounds of 'organic' compost. And don't tell the Excise, but you might find the odd pint of farmhouse cider consumed there too. 'Treasurer' Eddie will sort out your 'membership' of the 'club'.

USHA GUPTA

Blossom Hill Cottage • Born 17.6.62
(Souad Faress)

Usha is a solicitor and very comfortably off, as an equity partner with the **Felpersham** firm of Jefferson Crabtree. After several unsuccessful romances with apparently suitable men, this Hindu took a less obvious route and found growing happiness with the local vicar. **Alan Franks** even helped Usha mend her fractured relationship with her patrician father and depressive mother, who disapproved of Usha's move from Wolverhampton in 1991. Although she's well accepted now, integrating into **Ambridge** brought plenty of challenges, including a horrendous series of attacks by a gang of racist thugs. Relations with former friend **Shula Hebden Lloyd** never recovered from Shula's affair with Usha's then boyfriend Richard Locke, but Usha gets on very well with Shula's sister-in-law **Ruth Archer**. She relaxes through salsa dancing (with Ruth) and playing poker (with anyone foolish enough to underrate her).

NICOLA (NIC) HANSON

Hollerton
(Becky Wright)

Will **Grundy** started to go out with this single mother, of Jake (3) and Mia (1), in the summer of 2007. Nic was living in a small rented house after an acrimonious break-up with her unreliable (and unfaithful) partner Andrew. Having given up her job at Regal Coaches in Hollerton after the birth of Mia, Nic found herself caught in the 'benefit trap', with little incentive to return to employment. While **Eddie** was pleased to see Will moving on, **Clarrie** wished he could have found someone with less baggage. And **Emma** hated the arrival of a new woman in Will and **George**'s life.

BUNTY AND REG HEBDEN

Bunty born 20.2.22
(Sheila Allen)

Alistair Lloyd is in the unfortunate position of having an extra set of quasi in-laws – the grandparents of his adopted son **Daniel Hebden Lloyd**. Retired solicitor Reg and wife Bunty are the parents of **Shula**'s first husband Mark. Having had a bad experience in private education as a child, Alistair insisted that Daniel should go to the local state primary, against Reg and Bunty's wishes. But they won the second – and arguably most significant – round, siding with Shula and funding the boy through **Felpersham** Cathedral School, where he started in September 2006.

JOHN HIGGS

Loxley Barratt

Higgs – as most people know him – used to be general handyman and gardener at **Grey Gables**. He retired from the job in 2006 but continues to provide **silent** services as the chauffeur of **Jack Woolley**'s vintage Bentley.

HOLLERTON JUNCTION

Yes. I remember Hollerton —
The name, because one afternoon
(No seat!) the London train drew up there
Abruptly. It was late June.
The iPods hissed. Someone cleared his email.
No one left and no one came
On the bare platform. What I saw
Was Hollerton – only the name
*And '**Ambridge** – 6 miles', and grass,*
And Hassett Hills, and silage clamp,
And 'Services to Birmingham – Platform 2.
Wheelchair access via ramp.'
And for that minute a moped growled
Close by, and round him, noisier,
Farther and farther, all the cars
*Of **Borchester** and **Borsetshire**.*

With apologies to Edward Thomas

HOME FARM

STOCK

396 ewes • 115 hinds, stags, calves • 75 fattening pigs

CROPS

1,104 acres cereals • 148 acres grassland
100 acres oil seed rape • 60 acres linseed
80 acres woodland • 58 acres set-aside, including:
40 acres industrial rape • 10 acres willow (game cover)
4 acres strawberries • 6 acres maize

OTHER

25 acre riding course • Fishing lake • Maize maze

LABOUR

Brian Aldridge (managing and relief)
Adam Macy (deputy) • Andy, Jeff (general workers)
Tom Archer, **Jazzer** (pigs)
Students and seasonal labour
William Grundy (gamekeeper) • Fly (sheepdog)

With 1,585 mainly arable acres, Home Farm is the largest in **Ambridge** and carries out contract farming for **Brookfield**, the **Estate** and other local farms. As a partner in the Hassett Hills Meat Company, it raises and supplies high quality lamb to butchers and caterers, and sells its venison and strawberries at local farmers' markets.

CLIVE HORROBIN

A guest of Her Majesty
Born 9.11.72
(Alex Jones)

Many families have a black sheep. But when the family in question is the **Horrobins** then it gives a new dimension to the concept. Clive isn't prejudiced – he'll rob anyone, anywhere – but many of his illegal activities have been in the **Ambridge** area. These include an armed robbery on the **Village Shop**, after which he forced his big sister **Susan Carter** to harbour him (for which she served time), a string of burglaries on local homes and – worst of all – a vicious vendetta against former policeman George Barford which culminated in 2004 in a firebomb attack on George's house. Badly burned, Clive sought refuge with Susan once more, but this time she did the right thing. Clive got 12 years.

6, The Green, and elsewhere

Bert Horrobin isn't a 'glass half full' sort of bloke, and frankly it would take the powers of the most enthusiastic spin doctor to put a positive gloss on the fact that three of your six children *haven't* been to jail. **Clive**, Keith and **Susan** (now **Carter**) have all been on the wrong side of visiting time. Ivy (**Usha Gupta**'s cleaner at Blossom Hill Cottage) keeps her head down, hoping the others don't follow their siblings' example. Gary, Stewart and Tracy have managed it so far, although Tracy's attitude to work is pretty criminal, as several ex-employers can testify.

MAURICE HORTON

Borchester
(Philip Fox)

Butcher Maurice works part time at the business units at Sawyer's Farm making sausages for **Tom Archer**. He supplements this with work in a supermarket, and butchers the occasional venison carcass for **Home Farm**. Maurice was relieved to be able to give up his failing butcher's shop in **Felpersham** to work for Tom. It was there that **Eddie Grundy** found Maurice, when seeking a witness to mitigate the illegal meat case against him. Maurice was a bitter man and it wasn't until **Ed** interceded for his father that he agreed to give evidence. **Alistair Lloyd** later discovered that Maurice has a lot to be bitter about, as he had lost his previous business, wife and son through a compulsive gambling habit. Where did he discover this? The **Borchester** branch of Gamblers Anonymous, which had helped Maurice remain bet-free since 1995.

IZZY

Meadow Rise, Borchester
(Lizzie Wofford)

Ruth Archer had to put a few prejudices to one side when her daughter, the previously no-mates **Pip**, palled up with Izzy. While Pip's farm upbringing had kept her a child, Izzy seemed well into her teenage years by the time she was 12. But Ruth eventually saw beyond the crop tops and hooped earrings – and Izzy's home in the pretty rough Meadow Rise Estate – to see a sparky, confident girl with a welcoming nature and talent for music. Stepfather Dom is not only very taciturn but not a great earner, so Izzy's mum Karen works on a supermarket checkout and has two cleaning jobs to provide for the family, which includes 'mental' (Izzy's description) elder brother Keifer, younger half-sister Minnie and Ghengis the Alsatian.

JAXX CAFF

Borchester

The ubiquitous coffee-shop chains have introduced many Britons to the words 'skinny latte' (along with 'two pounds thirty for a cup of coffee?' and 'daylight robbery'). But most **Borchester** residents are happier with **Underwoods'** coffee shop and its consciously retro rival Jaxx Caff. To a soundtrack of 1950s pop classics, manager **Kenton Archer** and Frank the chef offer shoppers and local workers light meals and welcome refreshment. **Emma Grundy** and Polish waitress Otylia (Ottie) help part-time. But when Kenton is your boss that usually means you run the place.

JAZZER

Borchester • Born 1984
(Ryan Kelly)

It's easy to blame Jack 'Jazzer' McCreary for some of **Ed Grundy**'s wilder excesses. So let's do that. **Clarrie** certainly does. Joyriding, housebreaking and cannabis-growing are just a few of the offences to be taken into consideration. However, Jazzer does serve as an Awful Warning about the misuse of drugs – specifically ketamine, which left him a little clumsy and with memory problems. It also put paid to hopes of rock success in the now-defunct band Dross, with Ed, **Fallon Rogers** and Jazzer's elder brother Stuart. In recent years, though, Jazzer's knuckled down to early starts as a milkman on **Mike Tucker**'s round – and then onto his other part-time job looking after **Tom Archer**'s pigs at **Home Farm**. He has been known to arrive at Mike's cold store straight from a club. Careful with that milk van, Jazzer…

SATYA KHANNA

Wolverhampton

(Jamila Massey)

Usha Gupta's parents didn't want their daughter to move to the countryside, so for many years Auntie Satya was **Usha**'s main link to the parental generation. Satya often descends when she senses that Usha needs support, even if Usha doesn't want it at the time – although the accompanying food parcels are always welcome, as Usha isn't a great cook. After numerous failed matchmaking attempts, you'd think Satya would have been pleased when Usha fell in love with a prominent, pious and professional man. Unfortunately that man was **Alan Franks**, the local vicar, which didn't go down at all well with this practising Hindu.

OWEN KING

Under arrest
(Jonathan Keeble)

Owen worked as the chef at **The Bull** for **Sid** and **Kathy Perks** before being poached (as it were) by their arch rivals the Cat and Fiddle. When that pub closed, **Lower Loxley** took him on at their Orangery Café, where ironically he was once more to answer to Kathy in her new role as retail manager there. But the move was to go horribly wrong. When they both became involved in the 2004 **Ambridge** Christmas show, Owen took advantage of Kathy's friendly support and he raped her. He soon fled the area but in 2007, using the name Gareth Taylor, he was arrested for a similar offence. Kathy was forced to exhume her buried trauma as she faced the possibility of having to testify against him.

ALISTAIR LLOYD

The Stables
(Michael Lumsden)

Not everyone who plays the occasional hand of cards ends up threatening their marriage and mortgaging their house to pay their debts. But not everyone is a compulsive gambler. Suffocated by the stifling Archer clan and wife **Shula Hebden Lloyd**'s controlling nature – and under pressure following the loss of clients from his veterinary practice – Alistair found an outlet in poker. About £100,000 of his money also found an outlet, much of it to **Matt Crawford**. Alistair and Shula both had to accept some home truths as they rebuilt their marriage. Alistair refocused on his practice (which is based at Shula's riding stables) and his relationship with adopted son **Daniel**. Working together on **Ambridge**'s (unsuccessful) bid to win the Village Cup cricket competition helped too; Alistair is the Ambridge wicket keeper and captain.

DANIEL HEBDEN LLOYD

The Stables • Born 14.11.94
(Dominic Davies)

Daniel is the son of **Shula Hebden Lloyd** and (by adoption) **Alistair Lloyd**. His biological father was Shula's first husband Mark Hebden, who tragically died in a car crash without knowing that Shula was pregnant. Against Alistair's wishes, Daniel was sent to the Cathedral School in **Felpersham** in 2006. Daniel used to suffer from juvenile arthritis but his 'flares' of this nasty condition are becoming rarer. Indeed they may have ended altogether, so he has been more able to have fun playing cricket and horse riding – pursuits dear to his parents' hearts. He also helps Neil Carter with his pigs, which they find more inexplicable.

SHULA HEBDEN LLOYD

(formally Hebden, née Archer)
The Stables
Born 8.8.58
(Judy Bennett)

Shula's first husband Mark was killed in a car crash in 1994, unaware that after treatment for infertility Shula was pregnant with **Daniel**. Of **Jill Archer**'s twins, **Kenton** seemed to have the irresponsible gene and Shula the respectable one. But this regular churchgoer, bell-ringer and churchwarden, now running her own stables and riding school, once had a most unrespectable affair. Although **Usha Gupta** has still not forgiven her (it was with her then partner, Richard Locke) bizarrely her second husband **Alistair Lloyd** wishes Shula would remember it more often; then she'd perhaps be less judgemental of his own failings. Shula found that accepting her psychological contribution to Alistair's gambling problem was harder than making the financial contribution necessary to bail him out.

LOWER LOXLEY HALL

Few little girls now want to marry a prince and live in a castle. Perhaps they've been warned by the experience of **Elizabeth Pargetter**, who married a member of the landed gentry – **Nigel** – and was then landed with the exhausting joint responsibility for maintaining a 300-year-old mansion. To pay its way, the Hall takes conferences and sightseers. Nigel runs falconry courses and displays with falconer Jessica; the grounds boast rare breeds, cycle trails, an art gallery, a treetop walk and vines producing Lower Loxley's own wine. Staff include ancient retainers **Edgar and Eileen Titcombe**, volunteer guide **Bert Fry**, retail manager **Kathy Perks** and Hugh, the Orangery Café's chef. **Hayley Tucker** nannies for **Jamie Perks** and **Lily and Freddie**, and runs activity visits for schoolchildren. Elizabeth's advice to little girls? Stick to dreams of winning *Dancing on Ice*.

ADAM MACY

Honeysuckle Cottage • Born 22.6.67
(Andrew Wincott)

When unmarried **Jennifer** (now **Aldridge**) first became pregnant, she refused to name the father, although Adam's shock of red hair implicated local cowman Paddy Redmond. Jennifer's first husband Roger Travers-Macy later adopted the boy. After graduating in agricultural economics, Adam worked on farming development projects in Africa, returning to **Ambridge** in 2003. Despite his successful innovations at **Home Farm**, including a thriving soft-fruit business and an annual maize maze, he's had an uneasy relationship with stepfather **Brian Aldridge**. Adam is gay (and in a civil partnership with **Grey Gables** chef **Ian Craig**) and Brian can't help instinctively favouring Adam's half-sister **Debbie**. But the sibling rivalry was shelved as Debbie and Adam united in worry about Brian's plans for the future of the farm following the arrival of his love child **Ruairi Donovan**.

KATE MADIKANE

(née Aldridge)
Johannesburg • Born 30.9.77
(Kellie Bright)

In her younger and (much) wilder days, Kate caused little but trouble for parents **Brian** and **Jennifer Aldridge**: expelled from school, disappearing with travellers, having baby **Phoebe** at 19 and denying the father **Roy Tucker** his parental rights – until she needed to dump the child so she could 'find herself' in Africa, that is. She met husband **Lucas** on her travels and had his baby Noluthando ('Nolly') on 19 January 2001. Lucas has been a calming influence on her ever since. In 2005, when Kate returned from South Africa on one of her occasional visits, Roy found her much mellowed, so much so that his wife **Hayley** feared that there was a spark between him and Kate again. She need not have worried; that flame died a long time ago. Happy Kate and Lucas had their second baby – a boy, Sipho – in July 2007.

LUCAS MADIKANE

Johannesburg • Born 1972
(Connie M'Gadzah)

Cynics would say that **Kate** getting pregnant by a black South African was just another ploy to shock the more conservative elements in **Ambridge** (it certainly didn't go down well with her grandmother **Peggy Woolley**). But the match has proved a lasting one, even surviving their move from the pleasant surroundings of Cape Town to the more challenging environment of Johannesburg, when journalist Lucas took a job with the South African Broadcasting Corporation. Lucas married Kate in June 2001.

KIRSTY MILLER

Borchester
(Anabelle Dowler)

Chirpy Kirsty hasn't been desperately lucky with men in recent years. Her six-year on-off relationship with **Tom Archer** ended in 2005 when he fell for someone else – only for Tom to be dumped himself soon after he'd given Kirsty the 'big E'. While Tom eventually found happiness with Kirsty's best mate **Brenda Tucker**, Kirsty took up with the **Brookfield** herdsman Sam Batton – only to hear the 'it's not you, it's me' speech once again. (Sam was right, it was him: he'd fallen in love with **Ruth Archer** – but that's another kettle of rancid fish.) At least Kirsty didn't let the break-up with Tom sour her job at the family's shop, **Ambridge Organics**, where she works for Tom's sister **Helen**. Tom and Kirsty have managed to bury their past and are on good terms now when they meet at the shop or when she's working part-time at **The Bull**.

ELIZABETH PARGETTER

(née Archer)
Lower Loxley Hall • Born 21.4.67
(Alison Dowling)

The youngest offspring of **Phil** and **Jill Archer** often feels she's got the raw end of the deal. Some (especially her siblings) feel this is ironic considering she has a charming if eccentric husband in **Nigel** and lives in a Jacobean mansion. She's quick to point out that a colander is easier to keep afloat than **Lower Loxley** and that her main concern is for **Lily and Freddie**'s future. Apart from sibling rivalry, Elizabeth has faced some genuine challenges in her life. Before her marriage to Nigel, she had an abortion after being dumped by swindler Cameron Fraser; and her congenital heart problem required a valve-replacement operation after the birth of the twins. There's no doubt she's a fighter, which is probably just as well for Lower Loxley, given Nigel's frequent quixotic episodes.

LILY AND FREDDIE PARGETTER

Lower Loxley Hall • Born 12.12.99
(Theodore and Madelaine Wakelin)

When **Elizabeth** was pregnant with twins, the family feared for her life, as she was suffering the effects of a congenital heart condition. But Lily and Freddie were born – in that order – safely if a little early by caesarean section. **Hayley Tucker**, once their full-time nanny, still does the school run to and from Loxley Barratt Primary and looks after them in the holidays.

NIGEL PARGETTER

Lower Loxley Hall • Born 8.6.59
(Graham Seed)

Nigel has more fads than a Japanese fashion victim, but most of them have in some way added to the **Lower Loxley** visitor experience. Recent crazes included raising vines to make Lower Loxley wine, restoring a ha-ha and building a memorial to his eccentric great-uncle Rupert (from whom Nigel perhaps inherited his idiosyncratic charm). Increasing concern for the future we are bequeathing to our children (in his case to **Lily and Freddie**) led to Nigel forsaking his car and developing the Hall as an environmentally friendly stately home, insulated with sheep's wool (no, really) and offering 'green' weddings. It's just as well that Nigel has as his wife and co-manager the more pragmatic **Elizabeth**. His heart and her head combine to make Lower Loxley the success it is.

JAMIE PERKS

April Cottage • Born 20.7.95
(Ben Ratley)

Jamie lives with his mother **Kathy** and her boyfriend **Kenton Archer**, although being close (geographically and personally) to his father **Sid** he spends time regularly at **The Bull** too. Don't worry – Sid's the landlord there. Jamie's in the same year as **Daniel Hebden Lloyd**, although at different schools, so when they play together (if 12-year-olds still 'play') it's usually in **Ambridge**.

JOLENE PERKS

(neé Rogers)
The Bull
(Buffy Davis)

One definition of an intellectual is someone who can hear the *William Tell Overture* without thinking of the Lone Ranger. It could also be someone who can meet the landlady of **The Bull** without thinking of Dolly Parton, either because of her generous figure or her remarkably singable name. To be fair, that would be an entirely appropriate association, because Jolene (real name Doreen) still plays occasional gigs as a country music singer and pianist. Much of The Bull's success in recent years has been down to **Sid**'s wife, with line-dancing sessions, music nights and innovations including a cyber-area with internet access. Jolene's daughter **Fallon Rogers** has inherited her mother's musical ability, although you'd get a pretty withering look if you asked her to play country and western.

KATHY PERKS

(formerly Holland)
April Cottage • Born 30.1.53
(Hedli Niklaus)

With experience as a home economics teacher and at **The Bull** before her divorce from **Sid**, Kathy manages **Lower Loxley**'s café and shop, and organises occasional film nights at the village hall. She does her best to provide a stable and loving home for her son **Jamie**, with the erratic help of boyfriend **Kenton Archer**. The autumn of 2007 brought back a terrible trauma for Kathy, as she discovered that the man who had raped her at Christmas 2004 – former Lower Loxley chef **Owen King** – had been arrested for assaulting another woman. Facing bitter regret that she had not reported her assault, Kathy had to open up the wounds as she prepared to give evidence against Owen.

SID PERKS

The Bull • Born 9.6.44

(Alan Devereux)

Sid Perks is the nicest homophobe you could ever hope to meet. He runs **The Bull**, in which he has a 49 per cent share (with **Lilian Bellamy**), and is married to voluptuous **Jolene**. Sid's first wife Polly died in 1982. Their daughter Lucy and grandson Matt live in New Zealand while **Jamie** – his son from his second marriage – lives in **Ambridge** with **Kathy**. A keen cricketer for most of his life, Sid coaches at Loxley Barratt Primary and still takes an interest in the Ambridge team, despite his distaste at the gay **Adam Macy** being their star batsman. He was a driving force in their attempt at the Village Cup in 2007, and qualified as an umpire in that year as well.

HEATHER PRITCHARD

Prudoe, Northumberland
(Joyce Gibbs)

Once a mother, always a mother, but the distance from **Borsetshire** to Northumberland means that **Ruth Archer** doesn't get as much hands-on mothering as Heather would probably like. Widowed since 2002, Heather has a thriving social life and is quite comfortably off, as can be deduced from the number of cruises she takes.

ROBERT PULLEN

Manorfield Close • Born 13.7.15

A resident of **Ambridge**'s little plot of 'old people's homes', Bob Pullen is the son of a Black Country draper. He has many tales about the acts that he saw at Dudley Hippodrome as a young man, although little is known about the intervening decades. He's still a game old bird. Despite his notoriously weak bladder, he turned out for the 80th birthday celebrations of that youngster, HM the Queen, in 2006.

ELLEN ROGERS

Denia, Costa Blanca • Born 1926
(Rosemary Leach)

Nigel **Pargetter**'s aunt was younger sister to Nigel's deceased mother Julia. At Nigel's wedding to **Elizabeth**, ebullient Ellen revealed the hitherto concealed truth about her sister's humble origins. Julia loved to play the grande dame, so it was some surprise to find that she and Ellen were the daughters of a Lewisham greengrocer. Ellen has lived in Spain for many years, owning a bar in the ex-pat enclave of Denia. And let's clear up one possible area of confusion. Ellen is no relation to **Fallon Rogers**, although if they met we reckon they'd probably get on pretty well.

FALLON ROGERS

The Bull • Born 19.6.85

(Joanna van Kampen)

Fallon's trying hard to make it in the music business so, given the unforgiving nature of that scene, it's just as well she has ready access to work in **The Bull**, where she lives with mother **Jolene** and stepfather **Sid Perks**. Fallon's been musical director for a couple of local shows and has shown some talent as a promoter, running successful music nights in the function room 'Upstairs@The Bull', but ideally she wants her band, Little White Lies, to hit the big time. This is more likely (or less unlikely) than with Dross, her previous beat combo, which featured the vocal stylings of **Jazzer**, with **Ed Grundy** on guitar. They eventually got over their rancorous split, and in 2007 Fallon entered into a not-boyfriend-not-girlfriend-just-friends relationship with Ed. Until she started to fall for Ed, that is.

RONNIE

Farriers make a good living and are often popular with the ladies. We're not sure whether it was this or an interest in horse anatomy and metalworking which drew **Christopher Carter** to the profession. But in 2004 he managed to persuade Ronnie to take him onto the four-year long farrier's apprenticeship scheme.

GRAHAM RYDER

Borchester
(Malcolm McKee)

As a land agent working for the **Borchester** firm of Rodway and Watson, Graham used to supervise the management of the **Estate**'s 'in-hand' farmland. He was less than gruntled when **Matt Crawford** passed that role to **Debbie Aldridge** in 2006, leaving Graham with little more than collecting the quarterly rent from **Bridge Farm**. Graham can't quite understand why he is so unpopular in **Ambridge**. He sees himself as courteous and conscientious but others interpret that as oily and nit-picking. It's no wonder he wasn't elected to the parish council when he stood in 2003. The fact that he was widely regarded as Matt's placeman didn't help, either.

ST STEPHEN'S CHURCH

Established 1281

Despite this increasingly secular age, **Ambridge**'s fine church – whose history can be traced back to Saxon times – is still a focal point for the village. Indeed, it's a very significant one for some villagers, including **Alan Franks** (vicar), **Shula Hebden Lloyd** and **Bert Fry** (churchwardens), **Neil Carter** (captain of the bell-ringers) and **Phil Archer** (organist). If the sturdy walls could speak, they'd tell of considerable controversy in recent years; in particular the installation of a woman vicar, Alan's predecessor Janet Fisher. Of course, they can't speak. Just as well we've got **Susan Carter**, then.

SILENT CHARACTERS

One of the delights of **Ambridge** is that coterie of characters whom the listener knows well and can picture clearly but who are never actually heard to speak. A large but obviously rather quiet band, they include the ageing Mrs Potter and **Mr Pullen** at Manorfield Close; **Lower Loxley**'s gardener **Edgar Titcombe**, housekeeper **Eileen Titcombe**, resident falconer Jessica, chef Hugh and greenwoodworker Alec; **Eddie Grundy**'s friends **Baggy** and **Fat Paul**, and ex-friend **Snatch Foster**; semi-retired gamekeeper Malcolm, who assists **Will Grundy**; **Home Farm** workers Andy and Jeff; **Bridge Farm** dairy worker Colin Kennedy; exotic Anya at **Ambridge Organics**; waitress Otylia and Frank, who flips the burgers at **Jaxx Caff**; **Freda Fry**, who performs a similar function at **The Bull**; bell-ringer **Neville Booth** and his nephew **Nathan**; parish council chair **Derek Fletcher**; many of the **Horrobins**; and the fragrant **John Higgs**.

LYNDA SNELL

Ambridge Hall • Born 29.5.47
(Carole Boyd)

The years since Lynda and husband **Robert** arrived from Sunningdale in 1986 have seen a reduction in their circumstances but no diminution of Lynda's indomitable spirit. As Robert lost first his software business and then his career in IT altogether, Lynda started a job as receptionist at **Grey Gables** and later took in B&B guests at **Ambridge Hall**. All this while directing amateur dramatics, crusading on behalf of the environment (often to the irritation of the **Grundys** and local farmers), tending her garden (despite her annual hay fever) and caring for her pet llamas. The fact that they are named Wolfgang, Constanza and Salieri probably tells you all you need to know...

ROBERT SNELL

Ambridge Hall • Born 5.4.43
(Graham Blockey)

Retrenching after the collapse of his software business in 1995, Robert made a decent living with a few small clients and agency work. But when a contract was terminated in 2006 he started to despair of finding another job in the IT industry. To his – and most of his neighbours' – surprise, he found a late-late second career as **Ambridge**'s genial odd-job man. And in 2007 he became chief cook and guest-greeter when he and **Lynda** started to take in B&B guests. Genuinely in love with Lynda (he'd have to be), Robert has two daughters from his first marriage. The younger Coriander ('Cas') is a welcome occasional visitor to **Ambridge Hall**, while Leonie is more of the 'batten down the hatches' type.

CAROLINE STERLING

(née Bone, formerly Pemberton)
Grange Farm • Born 3.4.55
(Sara Coward)

An aristocratic bloom in the nettle patch that is **Ambridge**, Caroline found success in work – managing **Grey Gables** hotel – while suffering serial failure in love. She once had an affair with **Brian Aldridge**, although that hardly makes her unique among **Borsetshire** women, and her (eventual) first husband Guy Pemberton tragically died after only six months of marriage. But latter years have brought greater happiness, with marriage in 2006 to fellow hunting enthusiast **Oliver Sterling** and their purchase of Grey Gables from former owner **Jack Woolley**.

OLIVER STERLING

Grange Farm

(Michael Cochrane)

When Oliver arrived in **Ambridge**, after a divorce and the sale of his large farm in North **Borsetshire**, he was set for a gentle semi-retirement at **Grange Farm**, with a little hobby farming on 50 acres there. But, as joint master of the South Borsetshire Hunt, he met and fell in love with **Caroline**. They were married in 2006 and along the way became joint owners of **Grey Gables** hotel. This apparently conservative, establishment figure has proved to be a late-flowering radical, defying industry norms with a small herd of Guernseys supplying **Mike Tucker**'s milk round and producing an unpasteurised cheese – Sterling Gold. Radical too in placing his trust in herd manager **Ed Grundy**, despite the lad's tumultuous personal life and criminal record. Perhaps Oliver was compensating for his lack of parental investment in his real son and two daughters.

SABRINA AND RICHARD THWAITE

Grange Spinney

Well-heeled occupants of one of the most expensive developments in **Ambridge**. Richard commutes to work but finds time to turn out for the Ambridge cricket team. Sabrina is a super-fit 'yummy mummy', whose appearances at village events from pancake races to pub quizzes prove her to be fiercely competitive. She terrifies the life out of **Robert Snell**.

EDGAR AND EILEEN TITCOMBE

Lower Loxley

Who knew that such a bond was developing between the **Pargetters**' head gardener and their housekeeper (formerly Mrs Pugsley), previously noted mainly for their **silent** devotion to their duties. Following the death of Mrs Pugsley's long-estranged husband, Edgar Titcombe was thrown into teen-like angst until, encouraged by **Nigel**, he plucked up the courage to propose to the woman he had worshipped wordlessly for so long. They were married in 2006.

BRENDA TUCKER

The Nest, Home Farm • Born 21.1.81
(Amy Shindler)

Daughter of **Mike Tucker** and younger sister of **Roy**. In 2005, frustrated Brenda chucked in her job at Radio **Borsetshire** but her plans to improve her career prospects by taking a degree were set back by the death of her mother Betty. Getting a taste for commercial life through her involvement with boyfriend **Tom Archer**'s sausage business, she enrolled at **Felpersham** University in Autumn 2006 to study marketing. She supplemented her student loan by working for Tom and at **Jaxx Caff** until **Matt Crawford** spotted her potential and offered her vacation work, Alan Sugar-style, as his apprentice. As Brenda had previously tried to unveil Matt's role in a dodgy property deal and had been dumped by James Bellamy, son of Matt's paramour **Lilian**, this was a typically bold Crawford move.

HAYLEY TUCKER

(née Jordan)
Willow Farm • Born 1.5.77
(Lorraine Coady)

When she married **Roy**, Hayley naturally hoped for a little place of their own. But she reckoned without the stratospheric price of local housing, so they stayed at Roy's family home while saving every penny for a deposit. Hayley's other ambition – providing a baby brother or sister for Roy's daughter **Phoebe Aldridge** – also took a long time. Despite fertility problems, she was relieved to become pregnant in 2007 without expensive IVF treatment. A qualified nursery nurse, Hayley works at **Lower Loxley** as a nanny and runs activities for visiting school parties there. Bubbly and attractive Hayley still sees herself as an unmitigated Brummie. So since the death of mother-in-law Betty she's been rather surprised to find herself joint manager of an organic egg enterprise with neighbour **Neil Carter**.

MIKE TUCKER

Willow Farm • Born 1.12.49
(Terry Molloy)

Mike's had a tough life, so he could be forgiven for displaying a bit of a grumpy side. Made bankrupt as a dairy farmer in 1985, he took on a milk round at a time when doorstep deliveries were imperilled by the supermarkets. He also trained in forestry work, only to lose an eye in an accident. Then, tragically, in 2005 he lost his wife Betty. His slow recovery from the bereavement was helped by **Oliver Sterling**'s plans to supply local milk for local people. Mike now handles the processing at **Grange Farm** and buys the milk for his round, sharing the deliveries with **Jazzer**. Children **Roy** and **Brenda** know that he'd swap it all for one slow foxtrot with Betty again (they were great dancers) but they were pleased to see him come more out of his shell – even tentatively dating again.

ROY TUCKER

Willow Farm • Born 2.2.78
(Ian Pepperell)

Be-suited Roy is an efficient and popular deputy to **Caroline Sterling**. But the guests at **Grey Gables** could hardly imagine the colourful past of this capable manager. Once part of the group of racist thugs who terrorised **Usha Gupta**, Roy soon came to his senses and buckled down to business studies at **Felpersham** University. But while there, he had a daughter, **Phoebe Aldridge**, with **Kate Madikane** and fought for his right to raise the child. Following **Hayley**'s much-awaited pregnancy in 2007, the pressure increased on **Ambridge**-loving Roy to move from under the parental roof and find a home for his growing family.

UNDERWOODS

Well Street, Borchester

Underwoods department store –
It's the store with so much more!
Kitchen, bathroom, under stairs,
You'll find the things that you need there.
We have clothes for all of you –
Ladies, gents and children too
And the things to feed them all
In our well-stocked fine food hall.
Looking for a present, fellers?
Try our helpful perfume sellers!
Underwoods department store –
It's the store with so much more.

Advertising jingle (rejected)

THE VILLAGE SHOP

Ambridge is lucky to have an asset that many British villages have lost. More through philanthropy than anything else, failing **Jack Woolley** held on to the village shop and post office after he had sold all his other businesses. It's tried to move with the times, offering extended opening hours and DVD rental along with the more traditional groceries and emergency packets of tights. But could the best place to get up to date on village gossip be threatened by the Government's round of post office closures? Manager **Susan** 'Radio' **Carter** certainly hoped not.

WILLOW FARM

Two words denoting a rather complicated piece of real estate. Willow Farmhouse accommodates **Mike Tucker**, son **Roy**, Roy's wife **Hayley** and daughter **Phoebe Aldridge**. There are also eight acres owned by **Neil Carter** (the rest of the farm was sold long ago). Neil's land houses his outdoor breeding herd of pigs; an organic free range egg enterprise, run jointly with **Hayley**; and Ambridge View – **Susan**'s dream house which Neil self-built with Mike's help.

HAZEL WOOLLEY

California, Camden Town... who knows?
(Annette Radland)

Jack Woolley adopted the daughter of his second wife Valerie in 1972. Hazel claims to work in the film business but no one seems to know exactly what sort of films. She made one of her mercifully rare visits to **Ambridge** in summer 2005 and only left having failed to persuade Jack to sign **Grey Gables** over to her. **Peggy** loves her dearly, of course...

JACK WOOLLEY

The Lodge, Grey Gables • Born 19.7.19
(Arnold Peters)

As St Peter wrote, all flesh is as grass. Self-made Brummie businessman Jack Woolley dominated the **Ambridge** scene for four decades. But the onset of dementia in recent years forced him to divest his enterprises, selling **Grey Gables** hotel, the *Borchester Echo* newspaper and **Jaxx Caff**. The erratic progression of the illness means that Jack's (third) wife **Peggy** never knows whether the day will bring lucidity or lacunae. And the very occasional visits of Jack's adopted daughter **Hazel** (from his second marriage) usually make things worse. To finish as biblically as we started, how hath the mighty fallen...

PEGGY WOOLLEY

(formerly Archer, née Perkins)
The Lodge, Grey Gables • Born 13.11.24
(June Spencer)

Despite their middle age, Peggy still keeps a maternal eye on her children, **Jennifer Aldridge**, **Lilian Bellamy** and **Tony Archer**. Originally from London's East End, she is the widow of **Phil Archer**'s elder brother Jack, with whom she ran **The Bull** for many years. With a singular lack of imagination she married another **Jack (Woolley)** – in 1991. Although perhaps it's not surprising, given that her mother married two men named Perkins. Of a conservative bent in many ways, Peggy is one of the wealthiest women in the village. But, having lost her first husband to alcoholism, she's a living example that money can't buy happiness, forced as she is to cope stoically with her second Jack's decline due to Alzheimer's disease.